BACK TO SCHOOL IS COOL!

by Jim Jinkins

Level **2** Reader

Special thanks to Katonah Elementary School
and to Lewisboro Elementary School

Photography by Sandra Kress

Digital coloring and compositing by Paul Zdanowicz

Published by Dalmatian Press, LLC, 2012, Franklin, Tennessee 37067. No part of this book may be reproduced or copied in any form without written permission from the copyright owner. 1-866-418-2572

It was the first day
back to school
from summer break.
"Back to school rules!"
Pinky shouted.
"Back to school drools.
I'm not going,"
Tyler said.

Back to school
is cool!

He pulled the covers over his head.

"You are too," said Pinky.

"I am not," said Tyler.

"Tyler!

Hurry up,"

Mom shouted up the stairs.

"The big bus will be here soon!"

Tyler yelped and disappeared

somewhere in the laundry.

"Wow, Tyler,
you seem like you're . . .
what's that word
that means you're
really nervous and
totally worried?"
"Apprehensive?"
Tyler said from under
the laundry.
"That's it!"
said Pinky.
"That's the word
I'm looking for."

Oops!

"So you're apprehensive about the first day in the first grade?" Pinky asked.

All Tyler could do
was touch his nose—
which anybody knows means
Pinky was right on the nose.

Ap-ree-HEN-siv.
The "a" sound is like
the "a" sound in "apple."

Book of BIG WORDS

"That gives me an idea!" said Pinky.
"Are you going to make up one of your stories?" Tyler asked.
"Yesserooni positooni!" Pinky said.

"I'll just shut my eyes,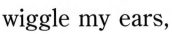

wiggle my ears,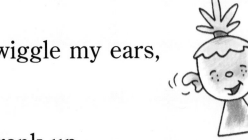

and crank up
my imagination,"
said Pinky.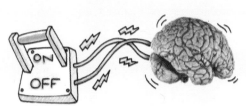

"The name of this story is . . ."

BACK TO SCHOOL IS COOL!

A made-up story by Pinky Dinky Doo

Told ya.

10

It was a no-big-deal,
regular day at
Great Big School.

NOT!

GREAT BIG SCHOOL

It was
School Picture Day.
It was the only day of the whole school
year when everyone wanted to look
their absolute best.

But that morning,

when Pinky looked in the mirror,

her hair looked like:

A A tornado
had hit it.

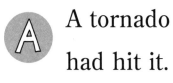

B Two cats had had a
fight on her head.

C It was spooky
haunted.

D All of the above.

The answer is **D**.

And **D** stands for Pinky Dinky's

Big Bad Hair Doo!

That is definitely a
Pinky Dinky Don't!

Pinky was worried
about having her picture taken
with such a bad hairdo!

But Pinky was not the sort
of person to lie down
when problems came up.
So she and Mr. G got busy.

At first Mr. G tried
to pull her hair up.

Then he
combed it down.
It worked for a
second, but then—

**BOI-YOI-
YOING!**

Pinky decided she
would have to wear
a hat to School
Picture Day.

At school,
Pinky noticed that
Nicholas Biscuit
was also wearing
a big hat.

The fake beard
made him look like
Abe Lincoln!

Normally,
Nicholas would comb
his hair into a pointy triangle.
But today his hair made
a quadrilateral.

Normally

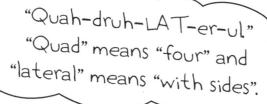

"Quah-druh-LAT-er-ul"
"Quad" means "four" and
"lateral" means "with sides".

Today

BOOK OF
BIG
WORDS

Pinky look around for Daffinee Toilette.
"Daffinee's hair is always perfect,"
Pinky said.
They found Daffinee.
Sure enough, her hair
was perfect.

That is,
until she turned sideways.

Behind the cutout
was a hairdo disaster!

When Pinky,
Nicholas,
and Daffinee
got to the classroom,
it looked empty.

Bobby "Broccoli-head" Boom

Everyone was hiding
because they
were all having
a bad hair day.

Abby McTrashy

Mookie "too much hair moose" Bazookie

Even Ms. Maganza and
Principal Dipthong
were having problems.

Ross
"Mophead"
Applesauce

And it was School Picture Day!
Everybody was reeeeally
apprehensive.

Pinky knew her friends were upset.
So she decided to Think Big!
Usually, Pinky had an everyday,
normal, kid-sized brain.
That is, until she decided to think big!
She thought

and thought

and thought.

This time as she
thought, her head
didn't grow any
bigger at all . . .
but her hair sure did.

Pinky Dinky's Hair Doo grew bigger
and BIGGER and BIGGER
until the classroom looked like
a shady rain forest.

WHOA!

JUNGLY!

SNIFF, SNIFF— this jungle smells like watermelon shampoo.

And then it happened...

Pinky had a big idea.

She said,

"Hey, I know what we can do . . .

 We can all shave our heads.

 We can knit our hair into sweaters.

C We can just GET OVER IT and have our pictures taken anyway!"

The answer was C, of course.

Everybody decided to just get over it and make the best of a bad hairdo situation.

They came out of hiding and took off their hats and hair cutouts.

Hey! I know that birdy!

Then they marched
to the gym,
where Mr. Pixel was waiting
to take their school picture.

And just as you might have guessed, that class picture was the funniest class picture ever taken.

Nobody ever expected
to end up laughing on
a Bad Hair Day.
But they did.
And nobody
was apprehensive
ever again.

"And that's *exactly* what happened . . . pretty much."

BEEP!
BEEP!
BEEP!

"Hey, that's the school bus," said Pinky.

"Oh, no," Tyler said.

"I don't want to go on the bus!"

"Come on, Tyler," Pinky said.
"You can sit next to me.
We ride the big school bus
together, remember?"
"Oh, yeah," Tyler said happily.

"Hurry up . . . ,"
said Pinky.

"Last one on the bus has
Big Bad Hair!"